ISBN 0-590-46404-3

Copyright © 1990 by Alan Baker.
All rights reserved. Published by Scholastic Inc.,
730 Broadway, New York, NY 10003, by arrangement with
Dial Books for Young Readers, a division of
Penguin Books USA Inc.

12 11 10 9 8 7 6 5 4 3 2   3 4 5 6 7 8/9

Printed in the U.S.A.   08

First Scholastic printing, March 1993

TWO TINY MICE

ALAN BAKER

SCHOLASTIC INC.
New York Toronto London Auckland Sydney

Two tiny
field mice,
look out
into the world.

They see
a soft,
furry rabbit
resting in
the sun,

a big March hare,

and a shuffling, snuffling mole.

They see
the shy,
little
sparrow
in its nest
of twigs,

and a sly,
old fox
far up
on the hill.

Two tiny
field mice
look again
and see

a croaking frog,

a quacking duck,

a weasel
at the
river's edge,

and a
muddy-brown
otter
swimming
in the water.

Two tiny
field mice
look
once more
and see

a bright-eyed,
gray squirrel
nibbling on
a nut,

a spiky,
spiny hedgehog
rustling through
the leaves.

But
do they see
two badgers,
playing
in the dark?

NO . . .

Two tiny field mice are home and sound asleep in their nest.